# Understanding Issues

# Smoking

## Gail B. Stewart

**KIDHAVEN PRESS™**

**THOMSON**
™
**GALE**

San Diego • Detroit • New York • San Francisco • Cleveland
New Haven, Conn. • Waterville, Maine • London • Munich

THOMSON
★
GALE
™

© 2003 by KidHaven Press. KidHaven Press is an imprint of The Gale Group, Inc.,
a division of Thomson Learning, Inc.

KidHaven™ and Thomson Learning™ are trademarks used herein under license.

*For more information, contact*
KidHaven Press
27500 Drake Rd.
Farmington Hills, MI 48331-3535
Or you can visit our Internet site at http://www.gale.com

LIBRARY OF CONGRESS CATALOGING-IN-PUBLICATION DATA

Stewart, Gail B., 1949–
  Smoking / by Gail B. Stewart.
    p. cm.—(Understanding issues)
Includes index.
Summary: Discusses smoking; the effects of smoking; smoking-related illnesses;
chemicals in cigarettes; and helpful ways to quit.
    ISBN 0-7377-1026-8 (hardback)
    1. Smoking—Juvenile literature. 2. Tobacco habit—Juvenile literature.
3. Tobacco—physiological effect—Juvenile literature. I. Title. II. Series.
  HV5733.S74 2003
  613.85—dc21

                                                 2002013084

Printed in the United States of America

# Contents

# Chapter One

# Who Smokes?

Tom is forty. He began smoking when he was thirteen. At first, he sneaked cigarettes from his mother's purse. Later, he bought them from a machine at the gas station near his house.

"It's the stupidest thing I've ever done," he says. "I bet everyone my age says that. But I really mean it, I really do. If I could do anything over in my life, I'd have not smoked that first cigarette."

## "What Are You Doing to Yourself?"

Tom is one of about 50 million Americans who smoke cigarettes. He would like to quit. He has tried many times. But it is a habit that is very hard to break.

"I've been smoking too long, I guess," he shrugs. "It's too hard to quit. I'm in a high risk group, too. My father and my brother got cancer. Both of them smoked. So I look at myself in the mirror some days and I ask myself, 'What are you doing to yourself?'"[1]

Some smokers do not have to ask themselves that question. Their families and friends ask them. Betsy, a mother of four, says that her daughter begs her to stop smoking.

"I feel like the world's worst mother," she says. "Melissa comes home from school with tears in her eyes. She's learned about smoking and how bad it is. She says, 'Why do you do that, when you know it could kill you?' And you know what? I don't really have an answer for that."

## Guilt

Betsy says she tried to keep her smoking from her children. She was not successful, however. "I smoke maybe two packs a day now," she says.

At first, when the kids were real little, I used to limit my smoking. I'd smoke on breaks at

Cigarette smoking is one of the hardest habits to break.

work, or when my husband and I would go out. I wasn't smoking more than ten cigarettes a day.

But then I started smoking more and more. I felt like I couldn't go all evening without a cigarette. So I'd tell the kids I was going for a walk. But I'd just go out by the garage and smoke. I felt like a little kid, sneaking around. Really, I didn't need to sneak. My kids could smell it on me. They'd say—"You're *smoking*?" Like they couldn't believe it.

But even with the guilt she felt, Betsy could not give up smoking. She would try, but she could never do it. Today she feels like she is not only letting herself down, but she is letting her children down, too.

What makes me really feel bad is that I tell my kids not to smoke. I tell them, I'm a smoker. I'm ashamed of myself. I can't stop smoking even though it's bad for me. I don't want you guys to be that way, too. But how can I tell them not to do something if I do it? Kids learn by watching. I can talk all day, but they won't remember my words. They'll remember mom lighting up a cigarette.[2]

## Starting Early

It is estimated that about one-third of the adults in the world smoke. That is more than 1 billion people.

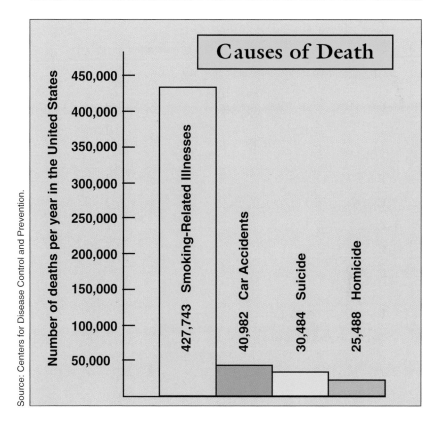

Source: Centers for Disease Control and Prevention.

But smokers are not only adults. Teenagers and pre-teens smoke, too. In the United States, as many as 6 million teens and 100,000 children under age thirteen are smokers.

That is a big part of the smoking problem, say experts. Almost nobody starts smoking as an adult. A person who is a nonsmoker at age nineteen will probably never smoke. The adults smoking today started when they were very young. And a person who starts smoking young will usually be a smoker for life.

"I started when I was eleven," says Juanita. "I'm thirty now, so I've been smoking nearly twenty years. Everybody I know tried smoking when they

A young smoker is likely to continue smoking into adulthood.

were young. That's when you start up. You know something funny? I never, *ever*, heard anybody say, 'Gee, I wish I'd started smoking.' No way. But you sure hear the opposite. They all say they wish they hadn't started."[3]

Celie agrees. She began smoking when she was only nine years old. She is twenty now, but says that she feels like she is an old lady.

I completely wish I'd never started smoking. I tried it when I was in third grade, and I just kept doing it. By the time I was in high school, I was smoking two packs a day. I couldn't have quit, I don't think. I didn't have the will power. But now I get up and I look at these lines around my mouth, and around my eyes. You know what that is? It's what old people's skin looks like. And that's from smoking. I mean, I'm twenty! I shouldn't

A child plays in a tobacco field. When children grow up around smokers, they are more likely to become smokers themselves.

have skin like this. I wish I'd never picked up a cigarette. I wish I'd learned to do something that was good for me, instead.[4]

## "He Was Always Saying He Would Quit"

Molly, sixteen, knows a good reason not to smoke. She never will, she says. That is because she watched her father die of lung cancer two years ago.

"He was always saying he would quit smoking," she says. "My mom and I would nag him about it all the time. He'd say, 'I know, I know.' But he couldn't quit soon enough, I guess. They found a spot on his lung when he had an X ray. They tried to operate on him, but the cancer had spread."[5]

Michelle's grandfather will die soon, too. He has been smoking since he was nine. He has a disease called **emphysema**, which makes it very hard for him to breathe.

He has been in the hospital it seems like forever. He can't get enough air in. He's so skinny, it's amazing he's still alive. He doesn't have the energy to sit up in a chair or talk to me. The doctor told my mom and dad that he will probably die soon. I get really sad about it. My mom says to remember he's the same Grandpa who used to take me fishing. But it's hard to remember that he used to be healthy. I try to remember, but I can't. I look at him lying there trying to breathe, and I can't.[6]

The nicotine in cigarettes is extremely addictive.

Lung cancer, emphysema, and other smoking-related illnesses are common causes of death among smokers.

## Why?

The risks are very scary. Each day about twelve hundred people in the United States die from smoking. Some, like Molly's father, die of lung cancer. Others get heart disease or other diseases such as emphysema.

Yet, people still smoke. More and more teens and children will start smoking. They are putting their health at risk each time they light a cigarette. The question is—why?

# Chapter Two

# Why Start?

In the 1950s scientists found proof that smoking was unhealthy. That is when experiments showed a link between lung cancer and smoking. Before that, people did not know the truth about the danger. The decision of whether or not to smoke was not based on health risks.

But today, people know. In school, children are taught about the dangers of smoking just as they are taught about drugs and drinking alcohol. Public service announcements on television and radio warn about the risks of smoking.

So why do young people ignore what they are taught, and begin smoking anyway?

## Curiosity

One reason is curiosity. Children see adults smoking and they wonder what it is like. Then one day, they try it themselves, just to see. Gilliam recalls her first time smoking:

> I tried it with my friend. We were walking to school, and he pulls out this pack of cigarettes.

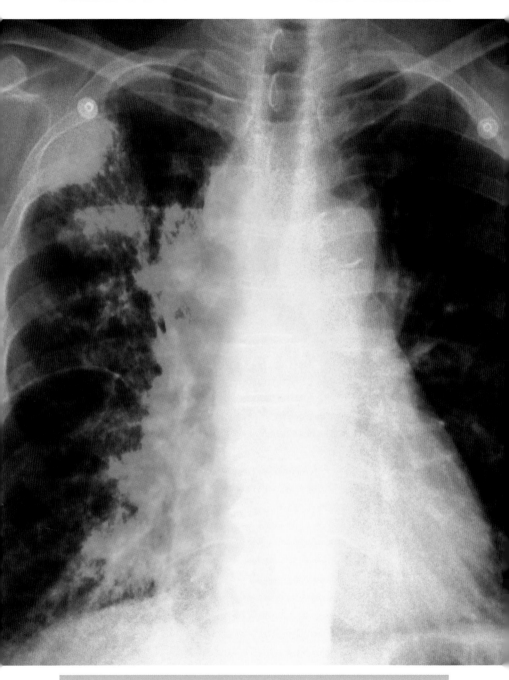

A chest X ray shows the diseased lung (in red) of a smoker who has cancer.

He found them in his dad's drawer. I think we were in fourth grade at the time. Anyway, he asked me if I wanted to try one. I was kind of scared, but it was exciting, too, you know? But I always wondered what smoke tasted like. I thought it must be pretty great, since everyone says that it's hard to stop. So we both tried it. We sat under some bushes behind somebody's garage. We smoked two cigarettes each. Oh—and we both felt pretty sick afterwards.[7]

## "I Always Thought It Looked Cool"

Experimenting with smoking often happens because a person wants to feel older. Ray, a thirteen-year-old boy, explains: "It's like driving. You see people doing it when you're little, and you think, I'm going to do that, too. My dad smokes, and I felt like when I started smoking I was more adult."[8]

"I always thought it looked cool," admits another boy, twelve. "You see guys that are tough—they're all smoking cigarettes. The movies, wherever. I think just about everyone who's supposed to look cool has a cigarette."[9]

Another boy, fourteen, agrees. He says that smokers have routines that he finds interesting.

"It's like a guy lights matches a certain way, maybe one-handed," he says. "That's cool. When you see somebody do that, you kind of figure they're cool. There's this one gangster movie, I can't remember it, but the guy smokes all the time. He doesn't even

Many young people start smoking because they think cigarettes make them look cool.

need to hold the cigarette. It's just in his mouth the whole time. That's cool."[10]

## "My Mom Would Faint"

Besides making them look older, young people often think smoking makes them appear independent or daring. They know that smoking cigarettes is a health risk and that it is illegal for anyone under eighteen. They are aware that their parents would probably be angry if they knew their children were smoking. Even so, young people are willing to take the risks.

Lucy, fifteen, admits that part of the fun of smoking is that it's illegal.

> Not just illegal, but *wrong*. In my house, nobody smokes. It's fun for me to smoke, because of that. Kind of being a rebel, you know? My parents don't have any idea that I smoke. Oh, God, my mom would faint if she knew! But that's what makes it kind of fun. It's fun knowing I have cigarettes in my purse. And my friends and I, we light up as soon as we go out. I'm not going to get cancer. I'm not going to smoke for a long time or anything. Just for awhile, while it's fun.[11]

## Feeling Comfortable

Many young people start smoking to fit in. Steve, twenty, says that is why he started. He and his family moved to Chicago when he was thirteen. He did not know any other kids, and was lonesome.

> I started hanging around with these guys after school. They smoked a lot. They'd go across the street from school, by this drugstore. I guess these guys were just hanging out, waiting for the late bus or something. I kind of started smoking then. I really didn't like it much. I knew my parents would be really mad if they knew I was smoking. But I didn't want to look bad in front of these guys, so I kept up.[12]

Often, young smokers say that smoking helps them relax when they are feeling pressured. "I got into a big fight with my dad," says Patrick, eighteen. "The first thing I did when I walked out of the house was smoke. It settled me down, I guess. It's just something that feels good when you're feeling stressed out."[13]

## A Habit

A young person may try smoking for many reasons. But one reason why smokers keep smoking is because it becomes a habit. They automatically reach for a cigarette at certain times.

Sometimes young people start smoking because they feel pressure to fit in.

"I need one after eating a meal," says Tom. "And every coffee break, I guess. I smoke in the car when I'm going to work. I smoke if I'm reading the paper. I really can't remember the last time I had coffee without a cigarette."[14]

Betsy says that when she is upset or nervous, the first thing she does is light a cigarette. "I don't know how I could stand it, being nervous without smoking," she says. "Maybe it's just something to do with my hands—who knows?"[15]

## From "I Want" to "I Need"

Once smoking becomes a habit, a person smokes more. Teens may start out smoking only a few cigarettes a week, but within a few months, they are smoking several each day. Their habit becomes much stronger every time they smoke.

"That's the **addiction** part of it," says one ex-smoker. "You don't just *want* to smoke—your body tells you that you *need* to smoke. When that happens, you're hooked.

"I remember that feeling. I suppose it's the same being addicted to drugs, or whiskey, or anything else. It's like, smoking isn't about relaxing with your buddies anymore. It's all about 'I need a cigarette, quick!'"[16]

Betsy says that she thought smoking was only a habit until she needed a cigarette first thing every morning.

For a long time, I'd just have a cigarette with my first cup of coffee. But then I didn't even

Many smokers spend a lot of time thinking about their next cigarette.

need the coffee. I know I've grown more and more addicted. It's hard to admit that. No one likes to feel that they are controlled by something. But I know cigarettes control me. I can tell by the number of cigarettes I need. I also know because I lie to myself. I bought another disposable lighter a few months ago. I told my-self that when that lighter was out of fuel, I would stop smoking. I promised myself. But last week I bought another one. I'm not stop-ping. I wish I could, though.[17]

## A Harmful Chemical

The cigarette itself is not what causes addiction. It is a chemical inside the tobacco, called **nicotine**. Unlike many of the other chemicals in cigarette smoke, nico-tine affects the brain. It can make a person feel more alert. It can also help calm a person who feels worried or anxious.

Tobacco plants are sprayed with many harmful chemicals that end up inside cigarettes.

The chemicals in a cigarette pollute the lungs like the smoke from a factory pollutes the air.

After lighting a cigarette, a smoker feels the nicotine effects right away. After the smoke is **inhaled**, or drawn into the lungs, the nicotine passes into the bloodstream. In just seven seconds the nicotine goes to the brain.

The effects of nicotine do not last long. As soon as a person finishes a cigarette, the level of nicotine in the bloodstream drops. That makes the person want to smoke another cigarette. Experts say that to keep the level of nicotine high, people need to smoke a cigarette every twenty minutes or so.

More and more nicotine means more and more cigarettes. All those cigarettes can cause many health problems.

# Chapter Three

# Thousands of Poisons

People may smoke to get the effects of nicotine. However, what they are getting is far more. Thousands of other ingredients inside a cigarette cannot be seen. Many of them can kill—and do.

## What Is Inside?

Cigarette companies add about seven hundred chemicals to their product. Some of these are poisons sprayed on tobacco as it is growing. The poisons kill insects and other pests that may damage the tobacco. However, these poisons are also very dangerous to people.

Once a cigarette is lit, it becomes even more dangerous. The heat of the burning tobacco releases about four thousand different chemicals. Some are the same poisons that are used to kill rats and mice. More than twenty are substances that are known to cause cancer. Each puff of the cigarette means more of these poisons are drawn into a smoker's lungs.

One sixteen-year-old girl says she was shocked when she learned that a well-known poison was found in cigarettes.

It was really gross. We got this list in our Healthful Living class. It had a whole bunch of the stuff that's in cigarettes, you know? And one of the top ones was **carbon monoxide**. I thought it was a misprint. I was like, "Isn't carbon monoxide the stuff that comes from car exhaust?" The teacher said that it was, and that carbon monoxide was in cigarettes—in large amounts.[18]

Carbon monoxide is a gas that cannot be smelled or seen. It is created by **combustion**, or burning. Cars give off carbon monoxide. Furnaces do, too. In tiny amounts, carbon monoxide is not dangerous.

Some smokers do not know what kinds of poisonous chemicals are in cigarettes and are usually surprised when they find out.

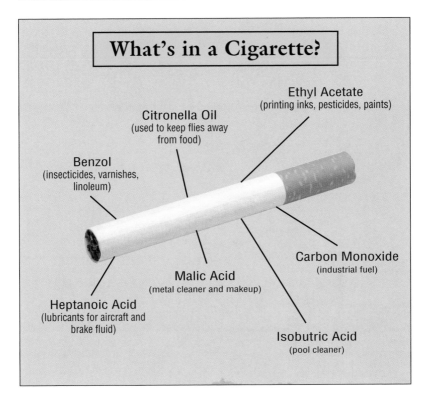

## What's in a Cigarette?

**Ethyl Acetate**
(printing inks, pesticides, paints)

**Citronella Oil**
(used to keep flies away
from food)

**Benzol**
(insecticides, varnishes,
linoleum)

**Carbon Monoxide**
(industrial fuel)

**Malic Acid**
(metal cleaner and makeup)

**Heptanoic Acid**
(lubricants for aircraft and
brake fluid)

**Isobutric Acid**
(pool cleaner)

But in cigarette smoke, the levels of carbon monoxide rise far beyond safe levels.

When the gas builds up in the bloodstream, the cells that carry oxygen in the blood cannot do their work. Without oxygen, smokers may get a bad headache. Often they feel nauseated, too, as though they have the flu. In a closed room where many people are smoking, the gas builds up even more. It can cause dizziness, blurred vision, and even heart attacks.

## Tar

**Tar** is another dangerous substance found in cigarettes. Tar is made up of thousands of chemicals that give flavor to cigarettes. Tests have proven that tar

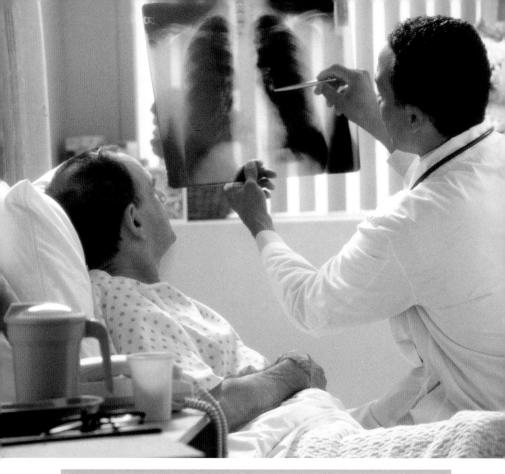

A doctor shows a lung-cancer patient an X ray of his diseased lung.

from cigarette smoke causes cancer in mice and in other laboratory animals.

The brownish black tar is sticky. When a smoker inhales, the tar collects in the smoker's lungs. The tar coats the tiny tubes in the lungs and makes it harder for a person to breathe. Smokers often have episodes of coughing, as their lungs try to get rid of the tar.

Doctors know that people who smoke are more likely to get diseases such as lung cancer and emphysema. Smokers also have longer-lasting colds and coughs than nonsmokers.

Tar has other effects, too. These are not as dangerous, but they are unpleasant. For instance, smokers get bad breath from the tar in cigarettes. Their teeth become yellow, too. Even their fingers become discolored from the tar in the cigarettes they hold.

## Nicotine

Besides making cigarettes so addictive, nicotine also has other dangerous effects. It raises a smoker's heart rate by up to twenty beats per minute after smoking a cigarette. Nicotine also raises the blood pressure. A fast heart rate and high blood pressure can be dangerous. The heart works harder than it should.

Ernest, seventy, had a heart attack eight years ago. He was told by his doctor that smoking is dangerous. Tests showed his blood pressure was too high.

"When I had my heart attack, I was more scared than I'd ever been," he says. "I kept thinking, I wish I could have one more chance. I would stop smoking, and I'd do everything the doctor said. And hey, I recovered. I haven't had a cigarette since April 22, 1994. And I'll never have another one."[19]

## Smoking and Cancer

Cancer is another serious risk. A smoker is about thirty times more likely than a nonsmoker to get certain cancers, such as cancer of the lungs, mouth, and **esophagus**. The longer a person smokes, the greater the risk.

Unfortunately, many young smokers do not worry about getting cancer. They tell themselves that they will quit long before they can get sick. But Donald says that they are foolish. He, too, believed that he was too young to worry about getting cancer.

"I've had part of my lung removed," he says. "They found I had cancer seven months ago. I'm not an old man—I'm forty-three. I have a daughter in eighth grade, and a son in sixth grade. I figured I'd cut down and quit before I turn fifty."

Donald's eyes fill with tears. "I don't know if I'll ever get to be fifty," he says. "I hope and pray I can.

The sticky tar in cigarettes causes a person's lungs to turn black.

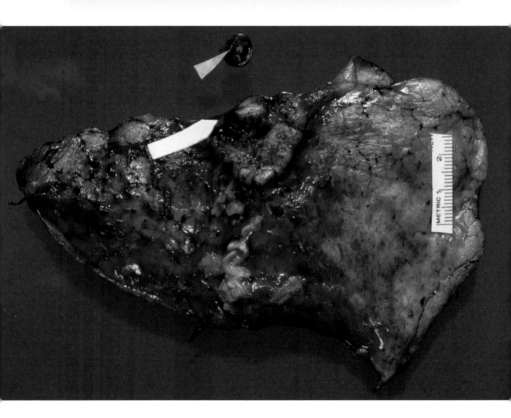

A young woman uses an inhaler to calm her asthma. Secondhand smoke is one cause of asthma.

I've had the treatments, and I've taken all the medications. I just want to live to watch my kids grow up. I can't believe I'm in this position now."[20]

## Passive Smoking

Smokers do not risk only their own health. Anyone else who breathes in smoke from their cigarettes can get sick, too. It is as if they were smoking—even if they have never had a cigarette. The smoke from someone else's cigarette is called **secondhand smoke.**

Secondhand smokers inhale the smoke that a smoker exhales. Even worse, secondhand smokers breathe in the smoke from a cigarette that is from the end of a burning cigarette. The poisons in that smoke are more dangerous because they are not filtered.

There are many victims of secondhand smoke. One study found that forty-seven thousand nonsmokers die each year from heart disease caused by secondhand smoke. Another three thousand die of lung cancer. Children are especially at risk. If a parent smokes, a child is twice as likely to have breathing problems such as **asthma**.

## Babies at Risk

The tiniest victims of smoking are unborn babies. Doctors know that when a pregnant woman smokes, her baby is smoking, too. Anything that goes into her bloodstream passes into the baby's bloodstream. That includes the thousands of chemicals in cigarette smoke.

The chemicals have the same sorts of effects on the unborn baby as they do on the mother. Nicotine makes that baby's heart rate go up. Carbon monoxide interferes with the amount of oxygen the baby gets, too. That means that the baby does not grow and develop as it should.

When Vonnie, seventeen, found out she was pregnant, she meant to stop smoking. However, seven weeks after the baby was born, she was still smoking.

I know it's bad. You see the cigarette pack, they have the warning right on the label. They tell

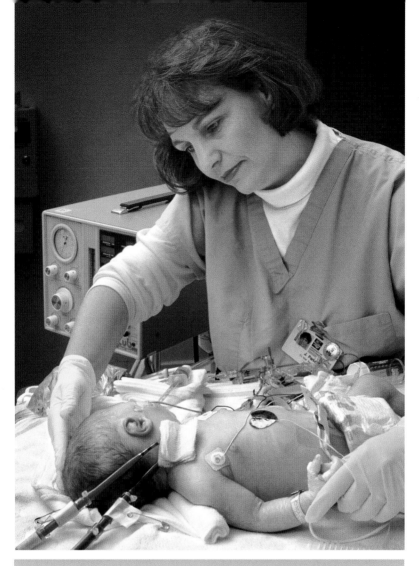

A premature baby born to a smoker is likely to have breathing problems throughout life.

you that you're hurting the baby if you smoke. My son was born six weeks too early. He's really small, and he is still in the [hospital] nursery. He gets help breathing because his lungs aren't developed all the way. I feel bad, I really do. I am going to stop smoking before I bring him home from the hospital.[21]

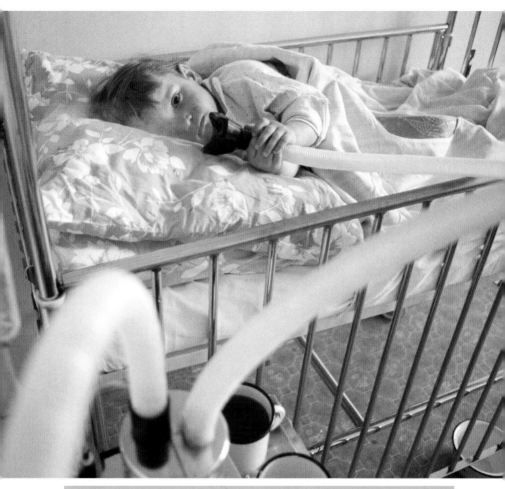

A child whose lungs were damaged by cigarette smoke relies on a breathing tube for oxygen.

With so many dangers for themselves and for the people around them, it is easy to see why many smokers want to quit. "It's hard though," complains one man. "I know it's bad for me. But I've tried a couple of times, and I can't stop. I wish somebody could just wave a magic wand, you know?"[22] Unfortunately, it is not that easy to quit.

# Chapter Four

# "I Have to Quit"

Greg, fifteen, is learning how addictive cigarettes can be. He is not a smoker. But his mother is. He says that watching her try to quit smoking has convinced him that he will never smoke.

"She smokes two packs a day," he says. "And the doctor told her she had to quit. She gets bad coughs all the time. She's tried two or three times before. But it never lasted.

"This time she threw away all the ashtrays and the lighters. She told my dad and my brothers and me that she is not going to smoke ever again. That was three days ago.

## "I Hope She Can Do It"

"One thing we all notice is how crabby she is. I know that's because she feels like she needs a cigarette. She also has a headache all the time. But the crabbiness is the worst."

Greg says that he and his brothers would rather have her be in a bad mood than have her smoke. "If she smokes she could get sick and die," he says.

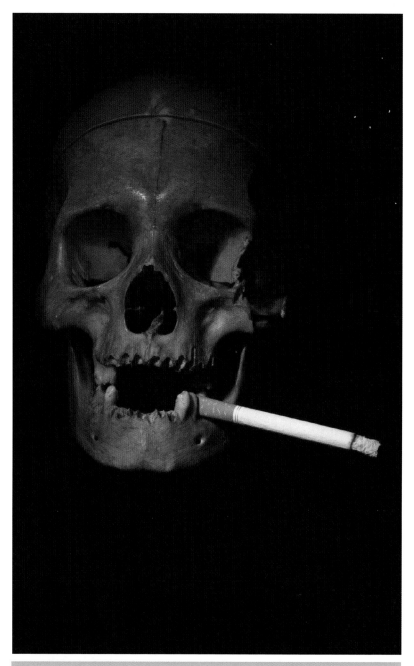

Nearly 450,000 Americans die each year from a smoking-related illness.

"There's a kid in my class whose mom died of cancer. That really made me feel bad. I don't want to have my mom die like that. We're all pulling for mom to quit. I hope she can do it."[23]

Those who have quit smoking say it helps to have the support of friends and family. Even so, it is a hard battle for many smokers. Even after a person has gone many days or weeks without smoking, the urge is often still there.

## Triggers

Karl, a former smoker, tells his story:

I stopped smoking thirteen years ago. And I haven't had a cigarette since then. I woke up one morning and just said to myself, "Today's

### The Benefits of Quitting

| | |
|---|---|
| 20 minutes | After quitting, a smoker's blood pressure and pulse rate reduce to normal, as does the body temperature of his feet and hands. |
| 8 hours | After quitting, carbon monoxide level drops and oxygen level rises to normal. |
| 24 hours | After quitting, the risk of heart attack decreases. |
| 48 hours | After quitting, a smoker's ability to taste and smell is enhanced. |
| 2 weeks | After quitting, circulation improves, walking is easier, and breathing efficiency increases by nearly 30 percent. |
| 1 year | After quitting, the risk of heart disease declines by 50 percent. |

the day you become a nonsmoker." It's like that guy says on the radio—"I'm sick and tired of being sick and tired." Anyway, that was me. I felt lousy all the time, especially in the morning. So I said I was going to stop. And that's what I did. But I'll tell you, it was hard. There are lots of times I almost gave in and smoked.[24]

Those who have given up smoking agree that it is a difficult battle. Many times a person will be tempted to smoke again. Certain situations trigger the urge to smoke, too.

"For me it was driving," says Ernest. "I always smoked when I drove, especially long distances. It seemed natural to light up, you know? The most natural thing in the world."[25]

Tina, who stopped smoking several years ago, says that what triggered her smoking was being with her friends. "That sounds awful," she admits. "But my friends all smoke. If I'm with them, I'm surrounded by smoke. It was sometimes all I could do not to just borrow a cigarette from my friends. One girl smoked the same brand as me, and that was especially hard."[26]

## Other Kinds of Help

Situations that trigger the urge to smoke can be a problem. Experts say that it helps for people to try to avoid smoking situations. But sometimes that is hard, too.

"I couldn't just stop seeing my friends," says Tina. "So I went to my doctor and told him how hard it

## An Expensive Habit

**What could you buy with $$ spent on cigarettes? ***

| purchase items | average price | approx. # per year | approx. # per week |
|---|---|---|---|
| Paperback Book | $7.00 | 260 | 5 |
| CD | $10.00 | 182 | 5 |
| DVD | $15.00 | 122 | 2-3 |
| Jeans | $30.00 | 61 | 1-2 |
| Video Games | $40.00 | 46 | 1 |

* Based on a smoker smoking one pack of cigarettes per day at $5.00 per pack.

was. It was getting so I didn't want to eat in the lunchroom at work. Anyway, he got me on a nicotine patch. It's just a small amount of nicotine that passes into your body. It isn't enough to hurt you or anything. But it makes that urge to smoke go away."[27]

Ernest has found that it helps to be around others who are quitting. "I joined a group of people at my church who are giving up smoking. It's like a support group, I guess. We just meet a couple of times each week and talk. It's kind of nice to hear that other people are going through the same things I am. We come up with ideas to stay smoke-free."[28]

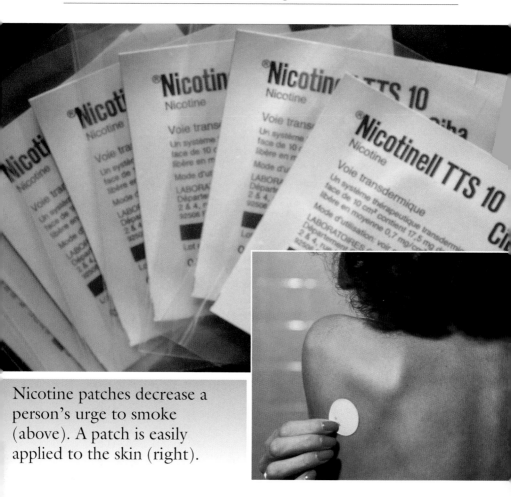

Nicotine patches decrease a person's urge to smoke (above). A patch is easily applied to the skin (right).

## Help for Quitters

Many people who are trying to stop smoking find that it helps to use a nicotine patch. It looks like a bandage. The patch releases a tiny amount of nicotine that passes through the skin into the bloodstream. It is not as much nicotine as a smoker would get from cigarettes. But it can help a person fight the urge to smoke.

"I wear mine on my inner arm," says one woman. "I can't say that I don't ever feel the urge to smoke. I do, several times each day. But the urges aren't as powerful.

I'm pretty sure that I can be stronger about not smoking with the patch. And once my body is out of the habit of needing cigarettes, I can stop using the patch."[29]

Some people chew special gum that contains a low amount of nicotine. Sherry, who has smoked for many years, had a problem using a nicotine patch. It made her skin red and sore. So her doctor told her to chew the gum when she felt the urge to smoke.

"This [nicotine] gum is great," Sherry says. "I wish they'd had this stuff years ago. My dad died of lung cancer twenty years ago. He tried and tried to stop smoking, but he never could. These new inventions like the patch and nicotine gum make it a lot easier, I think."[30]

A smoker who gives up cigarettes finds it is much easier to play sports and take part in other activities.

## "Good for You"

Quitting smoking is not easy. But those who have done it say it has made a big difference in their lives. They feel better. They do not get tired as easily. Their sense of taste and smell, which had been dulled by smoking, comes back, too.

Sam, a seventeen-year-old boy, is a former smoker:

I don't miss it. I stopped smoking last year. I stopped because I felt lousy, and because I realized how stupid it was. And now, I can tell you I'm glad I'm done with it. I don't miss all that money I was spending on cigarettes. I don't miss that cough that I had every morning, either. I never knew that it would make such a difference. But within a few days, I could tell I felt better.

I play soccer, and that means I run a lot. And even smoking a few cigarettes a day was making it hard for me. My heart was pounding out of my chest, just running a little. It's a bad, bad habit. Anybody who's thinking of starting it, think again. Anybody who's thinking of quitting it, good for you.[31]

# Notes

## Chapter One: Who Smokes?

1. Tom, interview by author, St. Paul, MN, August 1, 2002.
2. Betsy, interview by author, Blaine, MN, July 15–16, 2002.
3. Juanita, interview by author, Minneapolis, July 22, 2002.
4. Celie, interview by author, Minneapolis, February 1997.
5. Molly, interview by author, Crystal, MN, August 11, 1999.
6. Michelle, interview by author, Minneapolis, July 29, 2002.

## Chapter Two: Why Start?

7. Gilliam, telephone conversation with author, July 28, 2002.
8. Ray, interview by author, Blaine, MN, July 17, 2002.
9. Luke, interview by author, Blaine, MN, July 17, 2002.
10. Chang, interview by author, Blaine, MN, July 17, 2002.
11. Lucy, interview by author, Minneapolis, August 6, 2002.
12. Steve, telephone conversation with author, July 23, 2002.
13. Patrick, telephone conversation with author, July 29, 2002.

14. Tom, interview.

15. Betsy, interview.

16. Karl, interview by author, Minneapolis, July 26, 2002.

17. Betsy, interview.

## Chapter Three: Thousands of Poisons

18. Meghan, interview by author, Blaine, MN, July 17, 2002.

19. Ernest, interview by author, South St. Paul, MN, July 31, 2002.

20. Donald, interview by author, Minneapolis, August 1, 2002.

21. Vonnie, interview by author, Minneapolis, January 23–24, 1998.

22. Tom, interview.

## Chapter Four: "I Have to Quit"

23. Greg, interview by author, Columbia Heights, MN, February 17–18, 1996.

24. Karl, interview.

25. Ernest, interview.

26. Tina, interview by author, Blaine, MN, July 17, 2002.

27. Tina, interview.

28. Ernest, interview.

29. Gloria, telephone conversation with author, August 1, 2002.

30. Sherry, telephone conversation with author, August 13, 2002.

31. Sam, interview by author, Blaine, MN, July 18, 2002.

# Glossary

**addiction:** A habit that becomes a physical craving or need.

**asthma:** An illness that results in breathing problems.

**carbon monoxide:** A colorless, odorless poisonous gas that is created when a cigarette burns.

**combustion:** The act of burning.

**emphysema:** A dangerous disease that makes it very hard for a person to breathe.

**esophagus:** The tube that goes from the mouth to the stomach.

**inhaled:** Smoke drawn into the lungs by breathing.

**nicotine:** A substance in cigarettes that makes people become addicted. Nicotine also increases heart rate and blood pressure.

**secondhand smoke:** The smoke a nonsmoker breathes just by being around people who are smoking.

**tar:** A sticky substance in cigarette smoke that collects in the lungs. Tar can cause lung cancer and other problems.

# For Further Exploration

## Books

Gina De Angelis, *Nicotine and Cigarettes.* Philadelphia: Chelsea House, 1999. Good material on the addictive effects of nicotine, and how quickly it affects new smokers.

Arlene B. Hirschfelder and Arlene S. Hirsch, *Kick Butts: A Kid's Guide to a Tobacco-Free America.* Lanham, MD: Scarecrow Press, 2001. Excellent information about ways to decrease smoking in the United States.

Susan S. Lang and Beth H. Marks, *Teens & Tobacco: A Fatal Attraction.* New York: Twenty-First Century Books, 1996. Good interviews with young smokers. Also, a very good section on the chemicals in cigarette smoke.

Jillian Powell, *Why Do People Smoke?* Austin, TX: Raintree Steck-Vaughn Publishers, 2001. Excellent source, with a good section on the history of smoking.

## Websites

**Canadian Lung Association** (www.quit4life.com). This interactive site follows four young people trying to stop smoking. Excellent information on how a habit can become an addiction.

**Foundation for a Smokefree America** (www. tobaccofree.org). This site is geared for adolescents, and has heart-wrenching stories and photos of how tobacco can affect young people. Excellent information (including posters that can be downloaded) for school reports.

# Index

# About the Author

Gail B. Stewart has written over ninety books for young people, including a series for Lucent Books called The Other America. She has written many books on historical topics such as World War I and the Warsaw ghetto.

Stewart received her undergraduate degree from Gustavus Adolphus College in St. Peter, Minnesota. She did her graduate work in English, linguistics, and curriculum study at the University of St. Thomas and the University of Minnesota. She taught English and reading for more than ten years. Stewart and her husband live in Minneapolis with their three sons.